HORRiD HENRY'S
Holiday

HORRID HENRY'S
Holiday

Francesca Simon
Illustrated by Tony Ross

Orion
Children's Books

Horrid Henry's Holiday originally appeared in
Horrid Henry first published in Great Britain in 1994
by Orion Children's Books
This edition first published in Great Britain in 2009
by Orion Children's Books
a division of the Orion Publishing Group Ltd
Orion House
5 Upper Saint Martin's Lane
London WC2H 9EA
An Hachette UK Company

3 5 7 9 10 8 6 4

A catalogue record for this book is available from the British Library.

ISBN 978 1 84255 723 5

Printed by Printer Trento, Italy

www.orionbooks.co.uk
www.horridhenry.co.uk

*For Hannah Chissick, John Godber,
and Nick Winston — live and horrid!*

Look out for . . .

Don't Be Horrid, Henry!
Horrid Henry's Birthday Party

Contents

Chapter 1   11

Chapter 2   19

Chapter 3   31

Chapter 4   39

Chapter 5   45

Chapter 6   57

Chapter 1

Horrid Henry hated holidays.
Henry's idea of a super holiday
was sitting on the sofa
eating crisps and watching TV.

Unfortunately, his parents had other plans.

Once they took him to see some castles. But there were no castles. There were only piles of stones and broken walls.

"Never again," said Henry.

The next year he had to go to
a lot of museums.

"Never again," said Mum and Dad.

Last year they went to the seaside.

"The sun is too hot," Henry whined.

"The water is too cold,"
Henry whinged.

"The food is yucky,"
Henry grumbled.

"The bed is lumpy," Henry moaned.

This year they decided to try
something different.
"We're going camping in France,"
said Henry's parents.

"Hurray!" said Henry.

"You're happy, Henry?" said Mum.
Henry had never been happy about
any holiday plans before.

"Oh yes," said Henry.
Finally, finally, they were doing
something good.

Chapter 2

Henry knew all about camping
from Moody Margaret.
Margaret had been camping
with her family.

They had stayed in a big tent with . . .

comfy beds, a fridge,

a cooker, a loo,

a shower,

Oh boy!

said Horrid Henry.

a heated swimming pool,
a disco and a great big giant TV
with fifty-seven channels.

Bonjour!

said Perfect Peter.

The great day arrived at last.
Horrid Henry, Perfect Peter,
Mum and Dad boarded the ferry
for France.

Henry and Peter had never been
on a boat before.

Henry jumped on and off the seats.
Peter did a lovely drawing.

The boat went up and down and up and down.

Henry ran back and forth between
the aisles.
Peter pasted stickers in his notebook.

The boat went up and down and up and down.

Henry sat on a revolving chair and
spun round.
Peter played with his puppets.

The boat went up and down and up and down.

Then Henry and Peter ate a big
greasy lunch of sausages and chips
in the café.

The boat went up and down
and up and down and up and down
and up and down.

Henry began to feel queasy.
Peter began to feel queasy.

Henry's face went green.
Peter's face went green.

"I think **I am going to be sick**,"

said Henry, and threw up all over Mum.

"I think
I'm going
to be –"

said Peter,
and threw up all over Dad.

"Oh no," said Mum.
"Never mind," said Dad.
"I just know this will be our
best holiday ever."

Chapter 3

Finally, the boat arrived in France.
After driving and driving
and driving . . .

. . . they reached the campsite.

It was even better than Henry's dreams. The tents were as big as houses.

Henry heard the happy sound of TVs blaring, music playing, and children splashing and shrieking.

The sun shone. The sky was blue.
"Wow, this looks great," said Henry.
But the car drove on.

"Stop!" said Henry.
"You've gone too far."

"We're not staying in that awful place," said Dad.
They drove on.

"Here's our campsite," said Dad.
"A real campsite!"
Henry stared at the bare, rocky ground under the cloudy grey sky.

There were three small tents flapping
in the wind.
There was a single tap.
There were a few trees.
There was nothing else.

"It's wonderful!" said Mum.
"It's wonderful!" said Peter.

"But where's the TV?" said Henry.

No TV here, thank goodness. We've got books.

"But where are the beds?"
said Henry.
"No beds here, thank goodness,"
said Dad. "We've got sleeping bags."
"But where's the pool?" said Henry.

No pool. *We'll* swim
in the river.

"Where's the toilet?" said Peter.
Dad pointed at a distant cubicle.
Three people stood waiting.
"All the way over there?" said Peter.
"I'm not complaining,"
he added quickly.

Chapter 4

Mum and Dad unpacked the car.
Henry stood and scowled.

"Who wants to help put up the
tent?" asked Mum.

"I do!" said Dad.
"I do!" said Peter.

Henry was horrified.
"We have to put up our own tent?"
"Of course," said Mum.

"I don't like it here,"

said Henry.
"I want to go camping in the other place."

"That's not camping," said Dad.
"Those tents have beds in them. And loos. And showers. And fridges. And cookers, and TVs."

"Horrible,"
Dad shuddered.

"Horrible,"
said Peter.

"And we have
such a lovely
snug tent here,"
said Mum.
"Nothing modern
- just wooden pegs and poles."

"Well, I want to stay *there*,"
said Henry.

"We're staying here," said Dad.

"NO!" screamed Henry.

"YES!" screamed Dad.

I am sorry to say that Henry
then had the

longest
LOUDEST
noisiest
shrillest
most horrible

tantrum you can imagine.

Did you think that a horrid boy
like Henry would like nothing
better than sleeping on
a hard rocky ground in
a soggy sleeping
bag without
a pillow

?

You thought wrong.

Henry liked comfy beds.
Henry liked crisp sheets.

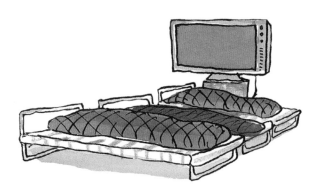

Henry liked hot baths.

Henry liked
microwave dinners,
TV, and noise.

He did not like cold showers,
fresh air, and quiet.

Chapter 5

Far off in the distance the sweet
sound of loud music drifted
towards them.

"Aren't you glad we're not staying in that awful, noisy place?" said Dad.
"Oh yes," said Mum.
"Oh yes," said Perfect Peter.

Henry pretended he was a bulldozer
that had come to knock down tents
and squash campers.
"Henry, don't barge the tent!"
yelled Dad.

Henry pretended he was a hungry *Tyrannosaurus Rex*.

"OW!" shrieked Peter.

Henry,
don't be horrid!

Mum looked up at the dark, cloudy sky.

"It's going to rain," said Mum. "Don't worry," said Dad. "It never rains when I'm camping."

"The boys and I will go and collect some more firewood," said Mum.
"I'm not moving,"
said Horrid Henry.

While Dad made a campfire, Henry played his stereo as loud as he could, stomping in time to the terrible music of the Killer Boy Rats.

"Henry, turn that noise down this minute," said Dad.
Henry pretended not to hear.

"HENRY!" yelled Dad.
"Turn that down!"

Henry turned the volume down the teeniest tiniest fraction. The terrible sounds of the Killer Boy Rats continued to boom over the quiet campsite.

Campers emerged from their tents
and shook their fists.
Dad switched off Henry's CD player.

"Anything wrong, Dad?"
asked Henry, in his sweetest voice.
"No," said Dad.

Mum and Peter returned
carrying armfuls of firewood.
It started to drizzle.

"This is fun,"
said Mum, slapping a mosquito.
"Isn't it?" said Dad. He was heating
up some tins of baked beans.

The drizzle turned into a downpour.
The wind blew.
The campfire hissed, and went out.
"Never mind," said Dad brightly.
"We'll eat our baked beans cold."

Chapter 6

Mum was snoring.

Dad was snoring.

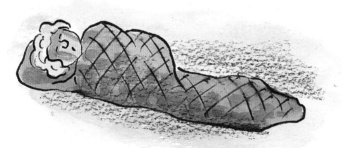

Peter was snoring.

Henry tossed and turned. But whichever way he turned in his damp sleeping bag, he seemed to be lying on sharp, pointy stones.

Above him, mosquitoes whined.

I'll never get to sleep, he thought,
kicking Peter.
How am I going to bear this
for fourteen days?

Around four o'clock on Day Five
the family huddled inside the cold,
damp, smelly tent listening to the
howling wind and the pouring rain.

"Time for a walk!" said Dad.
"Great idea!" said Mum, sneezing.
"I'll get the boots."
"Great idea!" said Peter, sneezing.
"I'll get the macs."

"But it's pouring outside,"
said Henry.
"So?" said Dad.
"What better time to go for a walk?"
"I'm not coming," said Horrid Henry.

"I am," said Perfect Peter.
"I don't mind the rain."

Dad poked his head outside the tent.
"The rain has stopped," he said.
"I'll remake the fire."

"I'm not coming," said Henry.

"We need more firewood," said Dad. "Henry can stay here and collect some. And make sure it's dry."

Henry poked his head outside the tent.

rain had stopped,
the sky was still cloudy.
The fire spat.

I won't go, thought Henry. The forest
will be muddy and wet.

He looked round to see if there was
any wood closer to home.
That was when he saw the thick, dry,
wooden pegs holding up all the tents.

Henry looked
to the left.

Henry looked to
the right.

No one was around.
If I just take a few pegs from
each tent, he thought, they'll never
be missed.

When Mum and Dad came back
they were delighted.
"What a lovely roaring fire,"
said Mum.

"Clever you to find some dry wood,"
said Dad.
The wind blew.

Henry dreamed he was floating
in a cold river . . .

He woke up. He shook his head.
He *was* floating. The tent was filled
with cold, muddy water. Then the
tent collapsed on top of them.

Henry, Peter, Mum and Dad stood outside in the rain and stared at the river of water gushing through their collapsed tent.

All round them soaking wet campers were staring at their collapsed tents.

Peter sneezed.

Mum sneezed.

Dad sneezed.

Henry coughed, choked,
spluttered and sneezed.

"I don't understand it," said Dad.
"This tent never collapses."
"What are we going to do?"
said Mum.
"I know," said Henry.
"I've got a very good idea."

Two hours later Mum, Dad,
Henry and Peter were sitting on
a sofa-bed inside a tent as big
as a house, eating crisps and
watching TV.

The sun was shining.
The sky was blue.

"Now this is what I call a holiday!"
said Henry.

More HORRID HENRY

Horrid Henry
Horrid Henry and the Secret Club
Horrid Henry Tricks the Tooth Fairy
Horrid Henry's Nits
Horrid Henry Gets Rich Quick
Horrid Henry's Haunted House
Horrid Henry and the Mummy's Curse
Horrid Henry's Revenge
Horrid Henry and the Bogey Babysitter
Horrid Henry's Stinkbomb
Horrid Henry's Underpants
Horrid Henry Meets the Queen
Horrid Henry and the Mega-Mean Time Machine
Horrid Henry and the Football Fiend
Horrid Henry's Christmas Cracker
Horrid Henry and the Abominable Snowman
Horrid Henry Robs the Bank

Horrid Henry's Joke Book
Horrid Henry's Jolly Joke Book
Horrid Henry's Mighty Joke Book
Horrid Henry Versus Moody Margaret

Colour books

Horrid Henry's Big Bad Book
Horrid Henry's Wicked Ways
Horrid Henry's Evil Enemies
Horrid Henry Rules the World
Horrid Henry's House of Horrors

Activity Books

Horrid Henry's Brainbusters
Horrid Henry's Headscratchers
Horrid Henry's Mindbenders
Horrid Henry's Colouring Book
Horrid Henry's Puzzle Book
Horrid Henry's Sticker Book
Horrid Henry's Mad Mazes
Horrid Henry's Wicked Wordsearches
Horrid Henry's Crazy Crosswords
Horrid Henry's Classroom Chaos
Horrid Henry's Holiday Havoc
Horrid Henry Runs Riot